CHRISTMAS

Songs
and Stories

The Big Treasure Book
of Christmas

GROSSET & DUNLAP · PUBLISHERS · NEW YORK

Copyright 1953, by Grosset & Dunlap, Inc.
All rights reserved under International and Pan-American Copyright Conventions.
Published simultaneously in Canada.   Printed in the United States of America.
ISBN: 0-448-00321-X   1973 PRINTING

As leaves that before the wild hurricane fly,
When they meet with an obstacle, mount to the sky,
So up to the housetop the coursers they flew,
With the sleigh full of toys, and St. Nicholas too.
And then, in a twinkling, I heard on the roof
The prancing and pawing of each little hoof.
As I drew in my head and was turning around,
Down the chimney St. Nicholas came with a bound.
He was dressed all in fur, from his head to his foot,
And his clothes were all tarnished with ashes and soot;

A bundle of toys he had flung on his back,
And he looked like a peddler just opening his pack.
His eyes — how they twinkled! his dimples, how merry!
His cheeks were like roses, his nose like a cherry!
His droll little mouth was drawn up like a bow,
And the beard on his chin was as white as the snow;

The stump of a pipe he held tight in his teeth,
And the smoke it encircled his head like a wreath;
He had a broad face and a round little belly
That shook when he laughed, like a bowl full of jelly.
He was chubby and plump, a right jolly old elf,
And I laughed when I saw him, in spite of myself;

A wink of his eye and a twist of his head
Soon gave me to know I had nothing to dread;
He spoke not a word, but went straight to his work,
And filled all the stockings; then turned with a jerk,

And laying his finger aside of his nose,
And giving a nod, up the chimney he rose;
He sprang to his sleigh, to his team gave a whistle,
And away they all flew like the down of a thistle.
But I heard him exclaim, ere he drove out of sight,
"Happy Christmas to all and to all a Good Night!"

—CLEMENT C. MOORE

FAVORITE

Pictures by
DELLWYN CUNNINGHAM

Music Arranged by
DOROTHY B. COMMINS

THE SPIRIT OF CHRISTMAS

EVERY year on December twenty-fifth we celebrate Christmas. For many days before Christmas there is a great deal of hustle and bustle. On Christmas Eve the Christmas tree is brought into the house. It is decorated with lights and stars and brightly colored ornaments.

On Christmas Day when the children wake up, they run to see what Santa Claus has brought them. Under the tree are many gifts, gaily wrapped with colored paper and ribbons. The whole family gathers together to open their gifts. Soon the house is filled with toys and wrappings and the chatter of happy children.

Then the family has a big Christmas dinner together. There are many good things to eat—turkey and plum pudding, and fruits and nuts and cakes of all kinds.

Christmas is the most wonderful holiday of the year. Do you know why? It is not just because Santa brings presents for everyone, but because he also brings the most wonderful gift of all—the gift of love and good will. On this day we promise ourselves that we will always help other people and love everyone. For this is the *true* Spirit of Christmas.

The Friendly Beasts

Jesus our brother, strong and good,
Was humbly born in a stable rude,
And the friendly beasts around Him stood,
Jesus our brother, strong and good.

"I," said the donkey, shaggy and brown,
"I carried His mother uphill and down,
I carried her safely to Bethlehem Town;
I," said the donkey, shaggy and brown.

"I," said the cow, all white and red,
"I gave Him my manger for His bed,
I gave Him my hay to pillow His head;
I," said the cow, all white and red.

"I," said the sheep with curly horn,
"I gave Him my wool for His blanket warm,
He wore my coat on Christmas morn;
I," said the sheep with curly horn.

"I," said the dove, from the rafters high,
"Cooed Him to sleep, my mate and I,
We cooed Him to sleep, my mate and I;
I," said the dove, from the rafters high.

And every beast, by some good spell,
In the stable dark was glad to tell
Of the gift he gave Immanuel,
The gift he gave Immanuel.

—Twelfth-Century Carol

JINGLE BELLS

James Pierpont

1. Dash-ing thro' the snow In a one horse o-pen sleigh,- O'er the fields we go — Laugh-ing all the way; Bells on bob-tail ring, — Mak-ing spir-its bright; What fun it is to ride and sing A sleigh-ing song to-night.

Chorus

Jin-gle bells! Jin-gle bells! Jin-gle all the way! Oh, what fun it is to ride In a one horse o-pen sleigh — Jin-gle bells! Jin-gle bells! Jin-gle all the way! Oh, what fun it is to ride In a one horse o-pen sleigh!

2. Day or two ago
I thought I'd take a ride,
And soon Miss Fannie Bright
Was seated by my side;
The horse was lean and lank,
Misfortune seem'd his lot,
He got into a drifted bank,
And we, we got upsot.

3. Now the ground is white,
—Go it while you're young;
—Take the girls tonight
And sing this sleighing song;
Just get a bobtailed nag,
Two-forty for his speed,
Then hitch him to an open sleigh,
And crack! you'll take the lead.

SANTA CLAUS'S WORKSHOP

THE whole year round Santa Claus lives at the North Pole, far, far away. He lives with Mrs. Santa and many Little Men who help him make all the wonderful toys that children find under the tree on Christmas Day.

Look at all the toys that Santa and his Little Men are making in their great workshop at the North Pole! Trains and airplanes, and donkeys to ride. Dolls and candy canes, drums and weather vanes. Horns and elephants, books and telephones. Saws are buzzing, machines are whirring—and the hammers keep pounding in Santa Claus's workshop. For three hundred and sixty-four days, Santa's workshop at the North Pole is the noisiest, busiest and happiest place in the world.

Then, just before Christmas, Santa sits down to read all the letters that the boys and girls send him. While his Little Men are busy finishing up the toys, Santa makes out his long list of names. On Christmas Eve, when all is ready, the toys are loaded onto the sleigh.

Santa climbs into his sleigh, shouts to the reindeer—and off he goes to bring toys to you and to all other nice children all over the world!

Silent Night

Words by Joseph Mohr, Translation anonymous

1. Si - lent night! Ho - ly night! All is calm, all is bright Round yon Vir - gin Moth-er and Child;

Ho - ly In - fant so ten-der and mild, Sleep in heav-en-ly peace, Sleep in heav-en-ly peace.

2. Silent night! Holy night!
Shepherds quake at the sight.
Glories stream from heaven afar,
Heav'nly hosts sing Alleluia;
Christ the Savior is born,
Christ the Savior is born.

3. Silent night! Holy night!
Son of God, love's pure light
Radiant beams from Thy holy face,
With the dawn of redeeming grace,
Jesus, Lord, at Thy birth,
Jesus, Lord, at Thy birth.

Away in a Manger

Words by Martin Luther

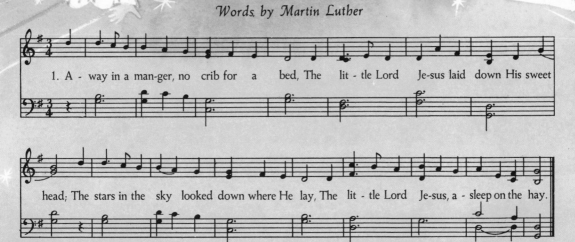

1. A - way in a man-ger, no crib for a bed, The lit - tle Lord Je-sus laid down His sweet head; The stars in the sky looked down where He lay, The lit - tle Lord Je-sus, a - sleep on the hay.

2. The cattle are lowing, the poor Baby wakes,
But little Lord Jesus, no crying He makes.
I love Thee, Lord Jesus! Look down from the sky,
And stay by my cradle, till morning is nigh.

3. Be near me, Lord Jesus, I ask Thee to stay
Close by me forever, and love me, I pray.
Bless all the dear children in Thy tender care,
And take us to heaven, to live with Thee there.

WHO IS SANTA CLAUS?

SANTA CLAUS is a jolly old man with twinkling eyes, snow-white hair and a long white beard. He wears a bright red suit trimmed with soft white fur, a cap to match, and shiny black boots.

Once a year on Christmas Eve, Santa Claus visits all the children. He rides through the skies in a sleigh drawn by eight tiny reindeer, with bells jingling on their harnesses.

Santa's sleigh is filled to the top with all kinds of toys for the children. Whenever he reaches a house, he takes a pack of toys on his back and carries them quietly into the house, or else he slips down the chimney. Then the reindeer quickly carry him off in his sleigh to the next house.

Boys and girls never, never see the real Santa Claus. But every year on Christmas Eve, they know that he is coming. So the Christmas tree is decorated and the children hang up their stockings.

On Christmas Day the children find their stockings filled with wonderful surprises and there are presents under the tree for all. Everyone loves Santa Claus!

CHRISTMAS IN THE HEART

It is Christmas in the mansion,
    Yule-log fires and silken frocks;
It is Christmas in the cottage,
    Mother's filling little socks.

It is Christmas on the highway,
    In the thronging, busy mart;
But the dearest, truest Christmas
    Is the Christmas in the heart.

Christmas Across the Ocean

ACROSS the ocean there are other lands and other children who celebrate Christmas, too. Many of them know Santa Claus by a different name. Some call him St. Nicholas or Good Old St. Nick. Some call him Kriss Kringle. The Swedish children believe that Santa's sleigh is driven by little mountain goats instead of by eight little reindeer. But, just like you, the children across the ocean know that Santa Claus will visit them on Christmas Eve and leave toys and presents for everyone.

On Christmas Day it is a lovely sight to see all the children with their different kinds of

presents. The happy Swiss boys and girls glide down the snowy mountain on long wooden skis. The children of Norway race across the ice on shiny ice skates, wearing red mittens to keep their hands warm. The Dutch boys and girls play with little toy windmills, and dolls that wear wooden shoes. The little French girls play with their new dolls, too. But the French dolls have long curls, big straw hats and they carry little baskets in their hands. Down in the warm land of Italy, Santa Claus leaves sailing ships and presents made of fine leather for the children.

Sometimes Santa brings the toys of one land to the children of another land. And when the children play with these new toys they have an especially good time. Because through all these toys, children of all countries say "Merry Christmas" to one another.

THE FIR TREE

FAR down in the forest, where the warm sun and the fresh air made a sweet resting place, grew a pretty little Fir Tree. Yet the little Tree was not happy. It wished so much to be tall like its companions, the pines and firs which grew around it.

"Oh, how I wish I were as tall as the other trees!" sighed the Fir Tree.

The Tree became so discontented that it took no pleasure in the warm sunshine, the birds, or the rosy clouds that floated over it morning and evening.

One winter, as Christmas drew near, many young trees were cut down, some even smaller and younger than the Fir Tree. These young trees were laid on wagons and drawn by horses out of the forest.

"Where are they going?" asked the Fir Tree. "They are not taller than I am. Indeed, one is much smaller. Where are they going?"

"We know! We know!" sang the sparrows. "We have looked in the windows of the houses in town, and we know what is done with them. They are dressed up in the most splendid manner. We have seen them standing in a warm room, adorned with all sorts of beautiful things."

"I wonder whether anything so wonderful will ever happen to me," thought the Fir Tree.

Another Christmas season arrived. This time the discontented Fir Tree was the first to fall. As the axe cut through the trunk, the Tree fell with a groan to the earth.

The Tree first recovered itself while being unpacked with several other trees in the courtyard of a house. It heard a man say, "We want only one, and this is the prettiest." Then two servants came and carried the Fir Tree into a large and beautiful room and set it up.

Some young ladies came and began to adorn the Tree. On some branches they hung little bags cut out of colored paper. From other branches were hung gilded apples and walnuts as if they had grown there. And more than a hundred little red, blue, and white candles were fastened to its branches. At the very top was fastened a glittering star made of tinsel. Oh, it was very beautiful! "This evening," they exclaimed, "how bright it will be!"

"Oh, that evening time were here," thought the Tree, "and the candles lighted! Then I shall know what else is going to happen."

At last the candles were lighted, and then what a glistening blaze of light the Tree presented!

And now the folding doors were thrown open and a troop of children rushed in. They were followed more slowly by their elders. The little ones shouted for joy till the room rang, and they danced merrily around the Tree, while one present after another was taken from it.

"What are they doing? What will happen next?" wondered the Fir Tree.

At last the candles burned down to the branches and were put out. Then the children received permission to plunder the Tree. Oh, how they rushed upon the Tree! Had it not been fastened by its glistening star to the ceiling, it would have been thrown down.

The children danced about with their pretty toys. But now no one noticed the Tree.

The Fir Tree looked forward joyfully to the next evening, expecting again to be decked out with lights and playthings, gold and fruit. "Tomorrow I shall not tremble. I will enjoy all my splendor," the Tree thought.

In the morning the servants came in. "Now," thought the Fir Tree, "all my splendor is going to begin again." But, instead, they dragged the Tree upstairs to the garret and threw it into a dark corner, and there they left it. "What does this mean?" wondered the Tree. "What am I to do now? It is terribly lonely here."

Then one morning people came to clear out the garret, and the Tree was pulled out of the corner. A servant dragged it out upon the staircase where the daylight shone.

"Now life is beginning again," thought the Tree. It was carried downstairs and into the courtyard. "Now I shall live," cried the Tree, joyfully spreading out its branches. But, alas! they were all withered and yellow. Only the star of gold paper, still stuck in the top of the Tree, glittered in the sunshine.

Several of the merry children, who had danced around the Tree at Christmas time, were playing in the courtyard. The youngest saw the gilded star and ran and pulled it off the Tree.

"Look what is sticking to the ugly old Fir Tree," said the child, treading on the branches till they crackled. Then a boy came and chopped the Tree into small pieces. The pieces were placed in a fire under the copper kettle, and they quickly blazed up brightly. The children came and seated themselves in front of the fire, and watched the Tree burn. Soon nothing remained of the Fir Tree but ashes.

The boys still played in the garden, and the youngest wore on his breast the golden star with which the Tree had been adorned. Now all was past; the Tree's life was past, and this story also— for all stories must come to an end at last.

O Little Town of Bethlehem

Words by Phillips Brooks

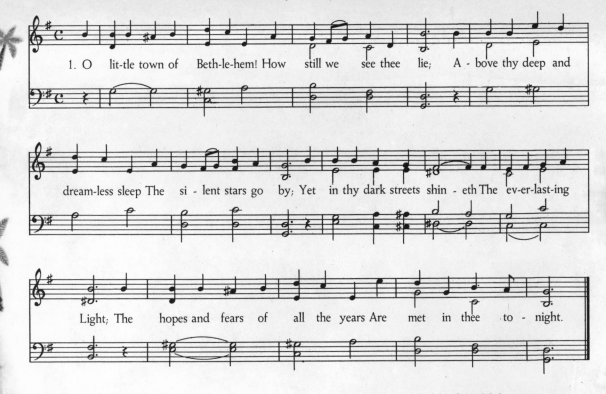

1. O lit-tle town of Beth-le-hem! How still we see thee lie; A - bove thy deep and dream-less sleep The si - lent stars go by; Yet in thy dark streets shin - eth The ev-er-last-ing Light; The hopes and fears of all the years Are met in thee to - night.

2. For Christ is born of Mary;
And gathered all above,
While mortals sleep, the angels keep
Their watch of wondering love.
O morning stars, together
Proclaim the holy birth!
And praises sing to God the King,
And peace to men on earth.

3. O holy Child of Bethlehem!
Descend to us, we pray;
Cast out our sin and enter in,
Be born in us today.
We hear the Christmas angels
The great glad tidings tell;
O come to us, abide with us,
Our Lord Emmanuel!

The Animals' Christmas

DO YOU know that the animals in the woods celebrate Christmas too? They do not have their Christmas tree in a house. But Mother Nature decorates a little fir tree that stands in a clearing in the forest. She dusts the tree with shiny snow and sprinkles bright icicles on the tips of the branches. Like magic, the plain little fir tree is changed into a Christmas tree that glistens and sparkles in the moonlight.

At midnight on Christmas Eve, all the animals creep out of their caves and dens. They gather around the fir tree to dance and sing together. The moose moos, the wildcat mews, the field mouse squeaks and the bear halloos. They have great fun exchanging fond Christmas greetings in animal language. Overhead the stars twinkle and the moon beams with pleasure.

Toward dawn Santa Claus rides swiftly by in his sleigh drawn by his eight tiny reindeer. "Merry Christmas, Santa Claus!" shout the animals. "Merry Christmas to all!" shouts Santa. The animals, too, love Santa Claus.

I Saw Three Ships

I saw three ships come sailing in,
On Christmas day, on Christmas day;
I saw three ships come sailing in,
On Christmas day in the morning.

And what was in those ships all three,
On Christmas day, on Christmas day;
And what was in those ships all three,
On Christmas day in the morning?

The Virgin Mary and Christ were there,
On Christmas day, on Christmas day;
The Virgin Mary and Christ were there,
On Christmas day in the morning.

Pray, whither sailed those ships all three,
On Christmas day, on Christmas day;
Pray, whither sailed those ships all three,
On Christmas day in the morning?

O they sailed into Bethlehem,
On Christmas day, on Christmas day;
O they sailed into Bethlehem,
On Christmas day in the morning.

And all the bells on earth shall ring,
On Christmas day, on Christmas day;
And all the bells on earth shall ring,
On Christmas day in the morning.

DECK THE HALL

Traditional Version   *Old Welsh Air*

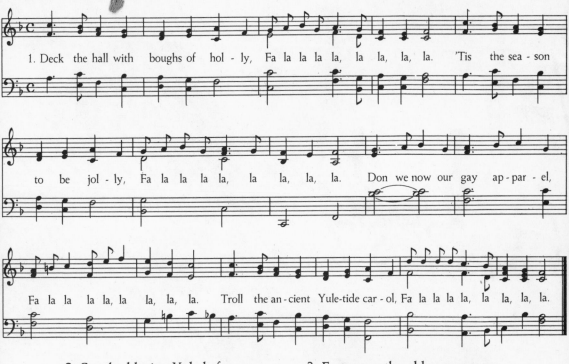

1. Deck the hall with boughs of hol - ly, Fa la la la la, la la, la, la. 'Tis the sea - son to be jol - ly, Fa la la la la, la la, la, la. Don we now our gay ap - par - el, Fa la la la la, la la, la, la. Troll the an - cient Yule-tide car - ol, Fa la la la la, la la, la, la.

2. See the blazing Yule before us,
Fa la la la la, la la la la.
Strike the harp and join the chorus,
Fa la la la la, la la la la.
Follow me in merry measure,
Fa la la la la la la la,
While I tell of Yuletide treasure,
Fa, la, la, la, la, la, la, la, la.

3. Fast away the old year passes,
Fa la la la la, la la la la.
Hail the new, ye lads and lasses,
Fa la la la la, la la la la.
Sing we joyous all together,
Fa la la la la la la la,
Heedless of the wind and weather,
Fa, la, la, la, la, la, la, la, la.

Tiny Tim's Christmas Dinner

SUCH a bustle ensued that you might have thought a goose the rarest of all birds. But then, to Bob Cratchit and his family, a goose dinner was very wonderful, especially to Tiny Tim, the youngest of the family. They were a happy family, for the Spirit of Christmas blessed their little house every day.

The older girls helped Mrs. Cratchit prepare the dinner and set the table. The two young Cratchits hustled Tiny Tim off into the wash house so that he could hear the pudding singing in the copper. Finally·dinner was ready and the whole family gathered around the table.

There never was such a goose. Bob said he didn't believe there was ever such a tender, tasty

goose cooked. It was steeped in sage and onion, and it was served with mashed potatoes and apple sauce. The family ate every bit of it, right down to the last bone on the plate.

Then Mrs. Cratchit left the room to take the pudding out of the copper and bring it in. Oh, what a wonderful pudding! Bob said it was the very best pudding she ever made. And it was just the right size, so that everyone had enough to eat. After dinner, apples and oranges were put on the table, and a shovelful of chestnuts roasted in the fire.

Then Bob proposed: "A Merry Christmas to us all, my dears. God bless us." Which all the family reechoed.

"God bless us every one!" said Tiny Tim, the last of all.

Adapted from *A Christmas Carol*, by Charles Dickens

The Nativity

LONG ago, in Galilee, there lived a gentle girl named Mary. One day an angel came to her and said, "Do not be afraid. You will have a son who will save the world."

Months later Mary went with her husband, Joseph, to Bethlehem to pay their taxes.

Since there was no room for them in the inn, they had to spend the night in a stable. There Mary's baby was born. Mary wrapped Him in swaddling clothes and laid Him in the manger. She called Him Jesus.

That same night there were shepherds watching their sheep on the hillsides near by. Suddenly a bright light shone around them and a voice said, "Do not be afraid. I bring you good news. Today

in Bethlehem a baby was born who is Christ the Lord. If you go to the city, you will find Him wrapped in swaddling clothes, lying in a manger."

Then other voices, like a choir of angels, sang, "Glory to God in the highest, and on earth peace, good will toward men."

The shepherds now were sure that angels had spoken to them.

They hurried to Bethlehem to see the child. There, in the stable, they found Mary and Joseph and the baby. Some donkeys and lambs stood quietly near the manger where Jesus lay. A light shone about Him.

Then the shepherds gave thanks to God, and went throughout the city telling all the people that Jesus was born.

But Mary stayed with her baby, and great joy was in her heart.

The Twelve Days of Christmas

On the first day of Christmas my true love sent to me a partridge in a pear tree.

On the second day of Christmas my true love sent to me two turtle doves, and a partridge in a pear tree.

On the third day of Christmas my true love sent to me three French hens, two turtle doves, and a partridge in a pear tree.

On the fourth day of Christmas my true love sent to me four calling birds, three French hens, two turtle doves, and a partridge in a pear tree.

On the fifth day of Christmas my true love sent to me five gold rings, four calling birds, three French hens, two turtle doves, and a partridge in a pear tree.

On the sixth day of Christmas my true love sent to me six geese alaying, five gold rings, four calling birds, three French hens, two turtle doves, and a partridge in a pear tree.

On the seventh day of Christmas my true love sent to me seven swans aswimming, six geese alaying, five gold rings, four calling birds, three French hens, two turtle doves, and a partridge in a pear tree.

On the eighth day of Christmas my true love sent to me eight maids amilking, seven swans aswimming, six geese